TWiN Magic

School Bully, BEWARE!

written by Kate Ledger   illustrated by Kyla May

SCHOLASTIC INC.

For Rori and Scarlett, my own magical twins!
-KL

With special thanks to Natarsha Larment, for dotting
the i's and crossing the t's. And to creative genius
Kyla May for breathing life into *Twin Magic* with
her abundant talent and impeccable style.

ISBN 978-0-545-48026-0

Copyright © 2013 by Mintie Moo Productions.

12 11 10 9 8 7 6 5 4 3 2 1   13 14 15 16 17 18/0

Printed in U.S.A.   40
First printing, August 2013

Lottie and Mia are twins.
Their best friend is named Toby.
He lives next door.

Mia wakes up early. She tidies her half of the room.

She picks out what to wear.

Then she packs her school bag.

Lottie slowly climbs out of bed.
"Hurry, Lottie! Toby's here!" Mia says.
"It's time to walk to school."
"I'm coming," Lottie says.
Then she rushes to get ready.

"Guess what?" Toby says.
"There's a new kid
in school today.
His name is Max."
"Really?" Mia says.
"I can't wait to meet him!"

SCHOOl

"Look," Lottie whispers.
"There he is!"
Mia smiles and waves at Max.
Max scowls back.
"He doesn't seem very friendly,"
Mia whispers to Lottie.

Soon it's time for Library.
Toby is first in line.
But Max pushes in front of him.
"Did you see that?" Mia whispers.
"That was not fair,"
Lottie whispers back.

Later, Lottie reaches for a book.
But Max grabs it.
"That's the book I want!" he shouts.

At recess the twins play foursquare
with Toby and Ben.
"I want to play, too," Max says.
"We already have four players," Toby says.
"You can play the next game."

"No!" Max shouts.
He grabs the ball
and kicks it as hard as he can.
It gets stuck up in a tree!

"That was really mean, Max," Toby says.
"If I can't play, then nobody can,"
Max says.
Lottie and Mia share a look.
They know how to get the ball back. . . .

"Hey, Toby," Mia whispers.
"Can you keep everyone busy?"
Toby is the only person who knows
Lottie and Mia's Super Twin secret.
"You can count on me!"
he says with a smile.

"**Abracadabra!**" Toby says.
He pulls a toad out of his pocket.
Soon more kids gather around.
Lottie and Mia smile.
Now it's time for . . .

...a little twin magic!
Lottie and Mia link their pinkie fingers
and whisper a magical charm:

"When TWINS get together,
we're stronger than ever!
TWin magic azam,
let's do what we can!"

Swoosh!

A cloud of sparkling dust
shimmers over the sisters.
They twirl around and turn into
magical Super Twins!

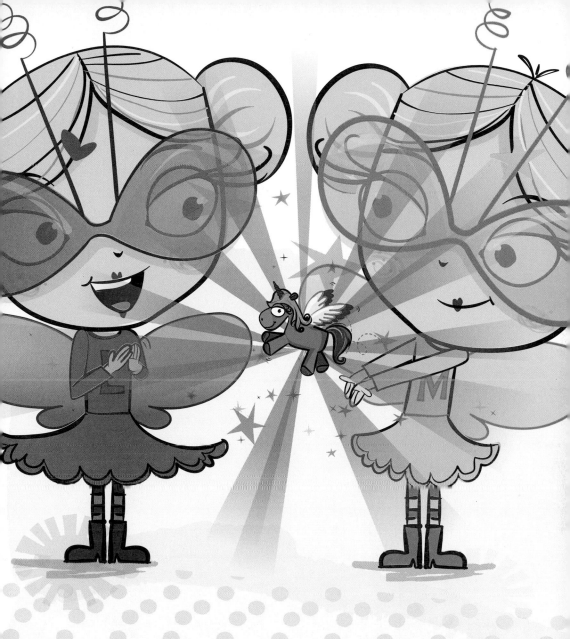

Mia giggles as something wiggles in her pocket.
"No need to fear! Rosie is here!"
a squeaky voice cries.
It's their magical friend, Rosie the unicorn!

"Hurry," Mia says.
"We need to get that ball!"
Rosie wants to help. She flies up to see
where the ball is stuck.
She is too small and weak to move it.

Lottie checks on Toby.
"Abracadabra!" he cries.
Toby pulls a flower out of his pocket.

"Nobody's looking,"
Mia says to Lottie.
The twins hold hands.
Together, Lottie and
Mia can move things
with their minds.

They think really, really hard
about the ball in the tree.
They feel their Super Twin magic
starting to work.
Their wings begin to flutter and buzz!

"Up here, Super Twins!"
Rosie cries.
The twins' feet lift off the ground.
They are making their wings flutter!
Lottie and Mia float up
toward the ball and grab it.

Rosie is so excited
that she does a flip!
Lottie and Mia flutter
down to the ground.

"Hurry!" Lottie says.
"We have to change back
before anyone sees us!"
Rosie flies back into Mia's pocket.

Lottie and Mia run over
to the other kids.
"Look what we found!" Mia cries.
"Hooray!" Toby cheers.
He winks at Lottie and Mia.

Max looks sad.
Lottie and Mia walk over to him.
"If you still want to play,
you can take my place," Lottie says.
"Or mine," Mia says.
"I can play in the next game."

"Thanks!" Max says.
"Sorry for being mean.
My first day is not going well."
"We thought you were a big bully,"
Mia says. "But you're not. Are you?"
"Nope!" Max says.

"Want to hear a funny joke?" Max asks.

"Sure!" Lottie says.

"Why did the cookie go to the doctor?" Max asks.

"Why?" Mia asks.

"Because he felt crumby!" Max says.

Everyone laughs, even Toby.

After that, everyone takes turns
playing together.
Lottie and Mia are glad
that Max isn't really a bully.
And they're super glad
to have made a **super** new friend!